Cinderella

retold by Stan Cullimore

Once upon a time, there was a girl called Cinderella. She lived with her two ugly sisters, Dippy and Dolly. They were horrible to Cinderella and made her do all the housework.

Poor Cinderella!

One day, Dolly saw something in the paper.

COURT NEWS

Prince sends out an invitation!

The handsome Prince Charming is looking for a wife. Tonight he is having a ball and he has invited all the ladies in the land. So the question on everyone's lips is: who will he choose?

Dolly put down the paper and ran to find Dippy. She was in the kitchen watching Cinderella doing the washing up.

"Dippy, quick, get your best dress on."

"Why?" asked Dippy.

Dolly explained about the ball.

"Have I got to have a bath too?"
Dippy asked.

Cinderella smiled. "The ball sounds wonderful. I can't wait to go."

Dippy and Dolly laughed.

"*You* aren't going," said Dippy.

"Why can't I go to the ball?" asked Cinderella.

Dolly snorted. "You've got work to do. I want you to scrub the floors, wash the windows and count my socks!"

"Besides, the Prince won't want to marry you when he sees US!" boasted Dippy.

The two ugly sisters spent the rest of the day getting ready for the ball. They washed their hair, put on lots of smelly make-up and got into their best dresses.

Help ME, Cinderella!

Cinderella, fetch my shoes!

It's not fair!

8

When it was time for the ball, the two
ugly sisters set off. Cinderella sat down
in the kitchen and cried.

Suddenly there was a puff of smoke,
a flash of light and a fairy godmother
appeared.

She smiled and said:

"Oh, Cinderella, don't be sad,
It really *isn't* all that bad.
My magic wand will set things right –
You *shall* go to the ball tonight!"

With that, the fairy godmother waved her magic wand. Cinderella's tattered old clothes immediately changed into a beautiful dress and her scruffy old shoes became a pair of delicate glass slippers.

"What lovely slippers!" said Cinderella. "Thank you." Then she frowned. "But how am I going to get to the palace?"

The fairy godmother smiled, then pointed her wand at a pumpkin. It changed into a magnificent coach.

?

Then the fairy waved her wand at the mice. They squeaked and grew and squeaked and grew and soon – they had grown into two fine horses!

Me – a horse?

Then the fairy godmother said:

"Now Cinderella, although I'm clever,
The carriage and horses won't
    last forever!
When the clock strikes twelve at the
    ball tonight,
Come home at once – or you'll be
    a sorry sight!"

So Cinderella jumped into the carriage and went to the ball.

When she got back home, the first thing she did was to sit down and open her diary ...

Tuesday 6th April

Dear Diary,

The ball was brilliant! I danced with Prince Charming the whole time. It was a bit embarrassing at the end though. I forgot to watch the clock. When it struck twelve, I had to run out of the palace so fast that I lost one of my glass slippers! Silly me.

The next day it was in all the papers that Prince Charming wanted to marry the mysterious girl who had left her glass slipper at the ball. He was going to search the land until he found her.

At last, there was a knock at the door of Cinderella's house. It was Prince Charming.

The Prince wants to marry me!

"The Prince wants to marry me!" beamed Dippy.

"No, he doesn't. He wants to marry ME — you can be bridesmaid!" snapped Dolly.

"You are BOTH wrong. It's Cinderella I want to marry," said the Prince.

"Rats!" said Dippy and Dolly.

So Cinderella married the Prince and they both lived happily ever after.

Rats!

As for Dippy and Dolly, they had to learn how to scrub floors, wash windows and count socks!

Serves them right!